Logansport-Cass County Public Library

LOGANSPORT LIBRARY

1501 9100 219 357 2

P9-ARC-344

J F BLA
What's this?
Blackstone, Caroline
Mockford

Logansport-Cass County Public Library

Logansport-Cass County Public Library

CLEO
ON THE MOVE

Caroline Mockford

Barefoot Books
Celebrating Art and Story

Logansport-Cass County Public Library

Cleo wakes,
Cleo winks.

Cleo yawns,
Cleo blinks.

Logansport-Cass County Public Library

What's happening today?
There are boxes everywhere.

Caspar sniffs,
Cleo frowns.

We're moving to another house.

It isn't far away.

Come and look!

We'll soon be there...

...now you can
run and play!

Cleo dashes,
Caspar chases.

Cleo wins the race.

There's so much here
to see and smell,

For Ned and Joe — C. M.
For Felix — S. B.

Barefoot Books
3 Bow Street, 3rd Floor
Cambridge, MA 02138

Text copyright © 2002 by Stella Blackstone
Illustrations copyright © 2002 by Caroline Mockford

The moral right of Stella Blackstone to be identified as the author
and Caroline Mockford to be identified as the illustrator of this work has been asserted

First published in the United States of America in 2002 by Barefoot Books, Inc.
All rights reserved. No part of this book may be reproduced in any form or by any means,
electronic or mechanical, including photocopying, recording, or by any information
storage and retrieval system, without permission in writing from the publisher

This book is printed on 100% acid-free paper
The illustrations were prepared in acrylics on 140lb watercolor paper
Graphic design by Jennie Hoare, England
Typeset in 44pt Providence Sans bold
Color separation by Bright Arts, Singapore
Printed and bound in Singapore by Tien Wah Press (Pte.) Ltd.

U.S. Cataloging-in-Publication Data:
(Library of Congress Standards)

Blackstone, Stella.
    Cleo on the move / [Stella Blackstone] ; Caroline Mockford. 1st ed.
[24]p. : col. ill. ;   cm.   (Cleo the cat)
Note: "The moral right of Stella Blackstone to be identified as
the author and Caroline Mockford to be identified as the
illustrator of this work has been asserted" [last page of text]
Summary: Cleo and her puppy friend Caspar move to a new home.
 ISBN 1 84148-898-4
1. Cats — Fiction. 2. Dogs — Fiction. 3. Friendship — Fiction.
4. Stories in rhyme. I. Mockford, Caroline. II. Title. III. Series.
[E] 21 2002   AC   CIP

1 3 5 7 9 8 6 4 2

Barefoot Books
Celebrating Art and Story

At Barefoot Books, we celebrate art and story with books that open the hearts and minds of children from all walks of life, inspiring them to read deeper, search further, and explore their own creative gifts. Taking our inspiration from many different cultures, we focus on themes that encourage independence of spirit, enthusiasm for learning, and acceptance of other traditions. Thoughtfully prepared by writers, artists, and storytellers from all over the world, our products combine the best of the present with the best of the past to educate our children as the caretakers of tomorrow.

www.barefootbooks.com

Logansport-Cass County Public Library